CREEP

A Collection of Poetry and Flash Fiction

Edited by
Tricia Reeks

Authors
Thomas I. Benton
Julia Burton
Terry Durbin
T. Kent
Kyle Richardson
Joshua Slone

Meerkat Press
Atlanta

Copyright © 2015

All rights reserved.

Creep is a work of fiction. Names, places, and incidents either are a product of each author's imagination or are used fictitiously. No part of this book may be reproduced in any form or by any electronic or mechanical means, without written permission from the author.

Rights to the individual works are owned by the author and each has permitted use of the work in this collection.

Published in the United States by Meerkat Press, LLC

ISBN-13: 978-0692378540
AISN: B00RPM9J4E

www.MeerkatPress.com

In Memory of Pandora

I have learned to not expect so much from others, only expect the best from me. That is living and it is a gift to behold. – Pandora

ACKNOWLEDGMENTS

Thanks to Esteban the zombie for inspiring this book. You'll be meeting the undead but oh-so-cool Esteban very soon—we hope you find him as irresistible as we did.

Thanks to Terry Durbin not only for giving us Esteban, but also for starting the fun little Halloween game on WritingForums.com that resulted in a large portion of the poetry in this collection. It was a month of ghosts, goblins, vamps, psychos, zombies, demons, and a host of other characters—many of whom appear in this book. They were all just too strange and wonderful to wither away in a virtual drawer someplace.

Thanks to WritingForums.com for being the coolest, friendliest, most generous community of writers on the internet. That's where we all met, and that's where we practice and hone our craft.

Thanks to Bernadette Geyer for her awesome poetry and copy-editing skills. She made our book so much better.

Thanks to our husbands, wives, girlfriends, boyfriends, kids, and pets for sharing us with the many interesting, weird, funny, scary, happy, sad, pretty, ugly, alien, and human characters and stories that take up space in our heads.

CONTENTS

Acknowledgments	i
Esteban the Zombie, by Terry Durbin	1
Curse of the Banshee Wind, by Julia Burton	2
I Love Halloween, by Terry Durbin	3
No Stranger, by Terry Durbin	7
White Horses, by Julia Burton	8
The Newcomer, by T. Kent	10
Cerberus Dreams, by Terry Durbin	13
Excerpts from Lillian's Journal, by Julia Burton	14
Nothing That Is Me, by Kyle Richardson	16
Hell Bent, by Terry Durbin	20
Ms. Stein, by T. Kent	22
Vamping Ain't Easy, by Marcellus Periwhimple (as told to Thomas I. Benton)	24
Cell #666, by Julia Burton	27
Five Kisses, by Terry Durbin	28
Still Life, by Joshua Slone	29
Memoirs of a Vampire Slayer, by Julia Burton	31

A Terrible Race, by Terry Durbin	32
Dear Zombie General, by Kyle Richardson	34
Malignant Desires, by Julia Burton	38
Something Wicked, by T. Kent	39
Zombies Rising, by Julia Burton	40
The Collector, by Terry Durbin	41
Just Beyond, by Joshua Slone	44
Dirge of the Dead, by Julia Burton	45
Country Ruffians, by Thomas I. Benton	46
Running Scared, by Julia Burton	49
Dear Mary, by Terry Durbin	50
The Perfect Match, by T. Kent	52
Inside My Head, by Terry Durbin	57
Under the Covers, by T. Kent	58
Bloodmoon Aria, by Julia Burton	59
Of Ritual, by Joshua Slone	60
The Old Ones, by Terry Durbin	63
Evil Secrets, by Julia Burton	64
Rockjunkie@Twitter, by Terry Durbin	65
Last Call, by Terry Durbin	68
Stewed, by Julia Burton	69

Mayhem, by Thomas I. Benton	70
By Any Other Name, by Terry Durbin	74
A Sinister Place, by T. Kent	75
About the Authors	76

◆ ESTEBAN THE ZOMBIE ◆

Terry Durbin

Esteban the zombie doesn't like meat,
No brains, no organs, no flesh will he eat.

Esteban the zombie has a sense of style,
Gucci, Armani, all laundered, not vile.

Esteban the zombie is always erudite,
No grunts as he kills you on Halloween night.

Esteban the zombie has but one rule,
"I may be undead, but I won't be uncool!"

◆ CURSE OF THE BANSHEE WIND ◆

Julia Burton

Near dark comes a gentle breeze
softly stirring grass and leaves,
but soon it grows in strength and might,
moaning, howling—causing fright,
breaking limbs and rattling doors
as it screams across the moors.

Banshee wind is on the prowl—
shrieking through the town, it howls.
Hold your babes, build up the fire
someone's raised the banshee's ire.

Secret deeds are brought to light
as the wicked wind takes flight.
In the morning, church bells ring,
death is the curse the banshee brings.

◆ I LOVE HALLOWEEN ◆

Terry Durbin

"I love Halloween, Daddy." The girl let go of the tall man's hand and skipped ahead down the sidewalk. The worn and dingy lace at the hem of her dress swirled around her ankles and her bare feet slapped lightly against the uneven bricks of the sidewalk.

"I know you do, Charlotte," he replied, stepping aside for a tiny pirate.

"There are so many treats!"

"But we must…"

"Yes, yes, yes," she chanted as she danced among the plastic heroes and grease-paint zombies. "Careful, careful, careful. Choose the sweetest sweet, but not just any treat we meet."

The tall man had to step off the sidewalk and onto the damp and dying October grass to avoid a somber parent studiously inspecting an apple. *How terrible*, he thought, *that such an innocent gift should be so mistrusted.* "That's right, dearest Charlotte," he said, bringing one long, thin finger to his lips and blowing lightly across its tip at the apple inspector. "I think it's fine," he whispered.

The little girl with the golden curls stopped in the middle of the walk, propped her fists on her hips and said, "But how will I know the very best treat?"

"You always know."

Behind him he heard the apple inspector mutter, "It's fine." There was a juicy crunch followed by a juicier scream that spun through the air like a purple maple seed until the tall man caught it in his pale hand and popped it into his mouth.

"I do, don't I?" Charlotte smiled. A boy in a Batman costume looked at her and she smiled wider showing more teeth. Many more. The boy began to cry. Charlotte snatched away the tiny pink bubble of his cries and licked the sticky sweetness from her palm with a black tongue. "I always do." Then she turned and ran a slalom through the maze of bag-carrying costumes.

And so it went that night as so many before it. An ageless child with hair the color of summer memories running through pools of streetlight gold playing Hide-and-Seek with the shadows of maple trees. From time to time she would see a likely treat and pause to watch as the cheerleader, or cowboy, or princess, or hobo would run in sugar-encumbered lightness down from a door checking to see what nugget had been added to a bucket or bag. She would sniff the treat with closed eyes, savoring the gingerbread-popcorn-chocolate aroma before deciding to dance on. Sometimes she would whisper in an ear and a puff of sweet fear-taffy would drift up and she would pluck it out of the air.

Watching Charlotte drift like a dingy cloud along the bricks in her earth-smeared dress doing her tricks-and-treats made the tall man happy. She called him 'Daddy' but he was no more her father than a scorpion is father to an asp. Their relationship was deeper than blood, more substantial than flesh. They were... of a kind. And they were forever, one Halloween at a time.

While Charlotte sampled and sought, the tall man gorged himself on the fruit of pain and anguish and lies and regret that escaped from every brightly lit house they passed like berries tumbling from a too-full bucket. On one porch a tiny cardboard-box robot shouted, "Trick or treat!" at a pleasant-looking woman standing in an open door holding a dish of candy. Smiling, she dropped two small candy bars into his plastic bag. Her gift to the tall man was much sweeter; to him she gave the saccharine bruises under her sweater, and the cotton-candy shame in her heart. From a man sitting alone in a parked car two doors down watching the children beg, the tall man tasted the heavy syrup of lust. Across the street, in the yard of a house painted the color of lemons, sharp edged shards of anger-brittle hung in the air like bits of shattered rock-candy pressed into the frosting of a hate-cake. Every house had its treat for him, and he fed his appetite with guiltless enthusiasm as he followed his companion.

Ahead, at an intersection where the brightly lit street was crossed by a darker and narrower lane, a pudgy scarecrow with a painted face stood under a streetlight looking sorrowfully into a bag with the face of a happy Jack-O-Lantern printed on its side. Charlotte danced toward him, around him like a dainty shark. Her choice had been made.

"What's the matter?" she asked.

"Not much chocolate," the scarecrow replied, still looking into his bag.

"What do you like best," Charlotte asked, stopping in front of him "Snickers? Milky Way?"

"Peanut butter cups mostly, but I ain't got any yet." He looked up at her and then down at her soiled dress and bare feet. "Wha'chou dressed up as?"

"What do I look like?"

"I don't know. You look old... no... not old. You look like... like... like a long time ago. You know what I mean?"

"Sure I do," Charlotte said, smiling her not-too-many-teeth smile, "and you're just right. I am a long time ago. Isn't that something? You got it right on the first try."

"I guess," the scarecrow said. "But where's your candy?"

"Oh, I'm just getting started. I was going to go get some fudge from this one house I know."

"Fudge? Nobody gives fudge no more."

"This house does."

"For real?"

"For real," she assured him. "Peanut butter fudge."

"Is it far?"

"Just around the corner, across the park." She pointed down the crossing lane.

"There's no lights on over there," the scarecrow said, squinting in the direction Charlotte was pointing. "You're supposed to have lights on if you're givin' out candy."

"This lady doesn't want too many kids to come. She can't make enough fudge for everybody." She shrugged her shoulders and started to walk toward the side street. "It's okay if you don't want to come."

"Wait," he said.

Charlotte stopped and looked back. The tall man loved her very much when she was hunting.

"And we'll be right back?" the scarecrow asked.

Charlotte drew an invisible 'X' on her chest with one finger. "Cross my heart and hope to die."

"Okay," he said. "Let's go."

The tall man leaned against the metal streetlight post and watched as Charlotte led the pudgy scarecrow across the street and into the darkness. While children and their parents moved from house to house behind him begging for sweets, he closed his eyes and waited for treats to fill the night.

He didn't have to wait long.

◆ NO STRANGER ◆

Terry Durbin

Me? I'm no stranger ... step closer and let me tell you my story.

Me? I'm just lonely ... take my hand and let's walk a while in the night.

Me? I'm not dangerous ... stop struggling and we'll get along fine.

Me? I'm not crazy ... ignore the blade in my hand.

Me? I'm not finished ... scream now, scream more.

◈ WHITE HORSES ◈

Julia Burton

Across the silver marshes,
under a vermilion moon,
sounds of ghostly white horses
racing over midnight dunes.

Silken manes and burning eyes,
hooves of polished steel,
drawn there by winds of death,
by a force against their will.

Breathing plumes of ash and smoke,
they rear and toss their heads,
to stare across a bloody sea,
at the Isle of the Restless Dead.

A child of fragile ivory bones,
rises from the heaving waves,
carrying bouquets of black lilies
to cover the tiny graves.

In secret they were buried,
hidden under piles of stone,
the wailing children waiting
for someone to take them home.

Sparks fly from polished hooves,
as the horses stampede in fright,
across the shifting dunes they run,
into the haunted night.

◆ THE NEWCOMER ◆

T. Kent

I pushed my way through the bodies shuffling about in front of the warehouse where we held our twelve-step meetings. The place was always packed the night after Halloween. Most holidays presented temptations to an addict, but for a Supernatural, Halloween was the worst. It was just so easy to blend in.

Inside, my friend Ozzie held court at the coffee machine, a cup of joe in his hand. He was addicted to the stuff like most everyone here, me included. Ozzie said it caused him many a restless day in his coffin—but the caffeine rush was worth it.

"Zeke, my man, you look like death warmed over," said Ozzie.

"Thanks, dude. Those threads are dope. What's the occasion?"

Ozzie wrinkled his nose at my mumbling zombie-speak. "I don't need an occasion do I? Not everyone can pull off the whole grunge thing like you do." Puffing his chest out, he ran his hands down the sides of his red velvet smoking jacket and smiled at a cute vamp across the room, fangs shining under the bright fluorescent lights.

Ozzie and I had very little in common past the absence of a beating heart and an extremely unhealthy addiction. Like most vamps, Ozzie was a player. Sure, he came here for the recovery, but that didn't stop him from chasing the ladies. As his sponsor, I spent half my time reminding him that relationships during the first year of recovery were a *big* no-no. Staying clean was hard enough without throwing the complications of love into the mix.

After pouring a cup of coffee, I looked over the usual selection of snacks and grabbed a handful of slimy grubs. Drool pooled at the corners of my mouth as I began to tremble and grunt with anticipation.

"You really are disgusting my friend," said Ozzie as he led us to the big circle of chairs.

I'd just settled in when I felt an elbow in my side.

"Watch it man, you're gonna knock another chunk of meat off my ribs."

But Ozzie wasn't listening. He had his eyes trained on the door where two chicks had just walked in. The one that had Ozzie's attention was a sexy young vampire with pasty white skin and long copper hair. She had on skin-tight gold satin pants and a low-cut black bustier. Boy did she have a set of jugs.

Next to her was… *Oh. My. God.*

Next to her was the ugliest zombie I'd ever laid eyes on. If my heart was still beating, it would have thudded its way right out of the smelly dead flesh of my chest.

She was young, dead maybe ten years if I had to guess from the amount of wispy black hair still on her head. She had the whole goth-grunge thing going on—from her muddy black combat boots to her tattered black t-shirt dress that said *Flesh-eater* boldly across the front. I felt guilty but couldn't stop myself from imagining the rotten peeling skin underneath.

Stop it already, you're acting like a damned vamp.

I watched her shuffle clumsily behind her friend as they found seats on the opposite side of the room. I wondered how long the young zombie had been clean, maybe not even a day based on her general state of dishevelment. If she stuck around she'd clean up her act like the rest of us. Hell, I'd even started washing my clothes once every six months.

"Fresh dead meat," said Ozzie. Then noticing my stare, he leaned over and whispered, "Tsk Tsk. It's not nice to gurgle over the newcomers."

Jerking at his words, I covered my mouth to stop the gurgling. I felt like I'd been caught with my hand in the organ donor jar.

I managed to straighten up haughtily in my chair for a good two seconds before my torso slowly listed to the right. I did envy vamps and faeries and all the other Supes who had control of their limbs.

"I'm not interested in her that way, wise-ass," I said, thankful that my dead skin hadn't flushed in years.

From the front of the room, Winchester, a cranky old ghost, said, "Okay, please, can everyone take a seat, and we'll get this meeting going." All the regulars had jobs at the meeting and Winchester's was to run the show. We had to put him to use somehow since he couldn't hold a broom or a coffee pot to save his life.

"Oswald, why don't you come up and read the twelve steps for us," said Winchester. He floated over to his seat at the front of the room.

As Ozzie stood up to go to the lectern, I couldn't stop myself from peeking over at zombie gal one last time.

Unholy shit. She was staring right back at me with those big dead eyes. As I watched mesmerized, the left side of her mouth lifted slowly in a lop-sided smile showing the rottenest teeth I'd seen in years. Damn, she was hot.

My mind, what was left of it, began to spin out one reason after another for me and zombie gal to hook up. Yeah, she was a newcomer, and yeah, I knew the rules. But since when did a respectable zombie care about the rules? A cup of coffee and a nice plate of road-kill after the meeting couldn't hurt. Just one concerned addict helping another.

From the front of the room Ozzie cleared his throat and began his reading of the twelve steps. His deep throaty voice instantly silenced every grunt, gurgle, and growl in the room.

"One. We admitted we were powerless over our addiction to humans and that our lives, deaths and everything in between, had become unmanageable…"

◈ CERBERUS DREAMS ◈

Terry Durbin

Cerberus sleeps,
and Hades' gates vomit out
the damned to walk like unanswered questions

connected to the not yet dead
where shadows touch heels.

One night,
only one night to collect regrets
like red and orange scales fallen from

the dragons of our lives
where intentions touch actions.

Make believe,
believe in plastic heroes
and synthetic demons dragging their thicker shadows

from house to house
where, beneath the cellars, Cerberus dreams.

❖ EXCERPTS FROM LILLIAN'S JOURNAL ❖

Julia Burton

I heard the panpipes playing
as I lay shivering in my bed,
my body trembled with dark desire
and my soul was chilled with dread.

My skin burned with wanton heat
as I lay in the blue moonlight,
bewitched by the lust I felt
on this wild enchanted night.

I fell into a restless sleep,
had dreams of strange desires,
of cloven hooves and polished horns
and caresses like molten fire.

I dreamed I ran through a twilight mist,
down to a secret glen
and hid behind a twisted tree
to catch a glimpse of him.

His skin was alabaster white,
horns polished silver bone,
hooves gold and cloven,
face like the gods of ancient Rome.

I dreamed that from the forest edge
there appeared a druid maid,
and she danced in the moonlight
to the panpipes that he played.

She let her garments slowly fall
revealing all her charms
and ran across the secret glade
and wrapped him in her arms.

He then picked her flowers
and twined them in her hair.
then swept her up in his arms
and carried her to his lair.

Amber lightening split the sky
and opened up a monstrous pit,
Cerberus from the abyss came forth
as the flames of hell were lit.

In the morning when I awoke
I found crushed flowers in my hair
and the aria that the panpipes played
drifted in the sultry air.

With the waning of the solstice moon
my belly began to swell,
protecting the seed that was spawned
when the beast escaped from hell.

666 was the demon's mark
on my unholy newborn son,
woe to all who survive this night—
something wicked this way comes.

◆ NOTHING THAT IS ME ◆

Kyle Richardson

It's four in the morning at Royal Memorial, and I've been dead a hundred and four years. These two facts aren't necessarily related. I have no idea what time I died. To be honest, I'm not sure what ended my life, either. Did I jump off a cliff? Was I sick? Did I succumb to a broken heart? All I know is—I'm dead. This much I'm sure. It's hard to think otherwise when you stroll around as transparently as I do.

That pear-shaped organ in my chest hasn't moved for over a century. Even the grass shows through my shoes. When I walk, not a single blade bends.

◆ ◆ ◆

The graveyard I haunt is peaceful. The lawn is always trimmed. The tombstones neatly polished.

I wave hello to the caretaker whenever he passes by. He keeps his head down, his eyes hidden behind the bill of an old ball cap.

His rusty lawnmower spits plant flecks through my trousers.

Sometimes I wonder, if I could speak, would anybody hear me? Would anyone care who I am? Or would my voice drift, unnoticed, to the barren edge of the earth—nothing but a cold whiff of air?

◆ ◆ ◆

I've never left Royal Memorial. The farthest I've travelled is to the northern edge, where the grass withers into dirt. On the other side of the dirt is a road. Beyond that, a forest of trees. Beyond the trees there's a city. I can see the buildings at night, their glittering tops jutting into the sky like candles.

Sometimes I try to get a closer look, but whenever I reach the dirt, something stops me. Like an invisible tether holding me in place. A leash that I can't see. I suspect that somewhere there's a knot, but I've yet to find where it is.

❖ ❖ ❖

On Friday night Herl tells me it's my death that's keeping me here. "You've been dead so long," he says to me, "you've forgotten how to live." His chubby face wrinkles like cellophane.

I kick at a granite tombstone. My leg vanishes and reappears on the other side.

"All the ghosts have moved to the city," he tells me. "Haunting the living—it's all the rage now! Anyone who's dead is doing it." He jabs an icy finger at my foggy blazer and says, "So why the hell aren't you?"

I imagine myself in the big city, leaping from a bathroom stall. My arms straight up in the air. A bowl of urine quivering behind my translucent waist. Nothing about this pleases me.

But before I can say anything, Herl drifts over the road and disappears into the woods. A milky balloon on the wind.

I stand with the tips of my loafers on the dirt, until the sun rises over the hills.

❖ ❖ ❖

On Saturday the caretaker doesn't show. Sick, maybe. Or perhaps he's given up.

Either way, I like this day the most.

The grass grows an extra millimeter. The tombstones dust, just a bit. Leaves tumble off the trees and scatter across the sun-baked plaques like paper doves. Nobody scoops them up. Nobody bustles them away. It's reckless and wild, these minuscule changes. Everything feels more alive.

I stroll through the wilderness of it all. From dawn until noon.

From noon until dusk.

I am forgotten. A nothing. A true waste of space. But today I feel almost real.

❖ ❖ ❖

Late in the evening, when the sky's flecked with stars, a vehicle parks on the road. The headlights flare like torches.

Cars are still new to me. These horseless carriages, their steel mouths groaning, their hooves rolling like balls along the asphalt. I'm not exactly a fan.

But the beings inside these metal beasts—they fascinate me. Flimsy and strange, they move like art. Like paintings come to life. The one that climbs from this car is no different. She slams the door with a robust twirl and the machine quickly goes silent. She trudges across the road, toward the dirt. Toward the grass.

Toward the nothing that is me.

I step back and sink into the trunk of an oak tree. Only my head sticks out.

The girl slumps against an old tombstone. Her clothes stick to her like paint. Denim trousers. A cotton blouse. A necklace twined from thin, dark rope.

Twenty-first century outfits look so uncomfortable.

She takes a deep, ragged breath and says, "I'm just so sick of it all, you know?" Her voice hovers in the air like mist. She brushes a lock of hair behind her ear. "Sometimes, I wish—" She shakes her head and looks up at her bangs, the water in her eyes glinting. "I don't know," she sighs. "I mean, what's the point of even living?"

I know this question isn't meant for me. No question ever is. This conversation is a private one, but I can't help answering. To myself. To the wind. To the nobodies and the nothings that will never hear, I say, "The point of living is to live. That's really the beauty of it."

The girl gasps and scrambles to her feet. She clenches a key in her fist. "I know karate," she says, her eyes narrowing, her gaze flicking between the lots. "I have a gun." She turns and jabs the air to show she means business. "And a knife." She waits, for a moment, while the wind whips her hair, then says, quietly, "Who's there?"

For the first time in a hundred and four years, that pear-shaped organ in my chest moves. Just a little.

Beneath me, a blade of grass bends.

❖ HELL BENT ❖

Terry Durbin

Into the desert night I drive,
Speedometer pegged at ninety-five.
A hell-bound truck right on my tail,
My ears are filled with its engine's wail.

Or are those the cries of its doomed load
Of souls collected along this road?
Other victims just like me
Crushed under the wheels of the truck I see.

Ever closer does the Leviathan creep,
As its sanguine headlights make me weep.
Tears flow like prayers from my eyes,
'Neath silent, black, midnight skies.

A towering monster bearing down,
Sixty miles from the nearest town.
My fragile car is running on fumes,
In moments I know I'll meet my doom.

Asphalt screams under my tires,
But the truck is driven by hell's own fires.
Up ahead the road like a serpent bends.
I know that's where my story ends.

A thump from behind pushes me ahead,
Across desert stones I'll soon be spread.
The radio comes on—not my choice—
And the laugh I hear is Satan's voice.

◈ MS. STEIN ◈

T. Kent

Ms. Stein touched red
to lips and cheeks
a bit of color
turned bleak to chic

She curled and teased
her long black hair
its platinum streaks
were dyed with care

A long sleeved dress
her favorite thing
to cover scars
stitched up with string

She sprayed perfume
her smell it masked
then checked her purse
for keys and cash

She flipped through
cards of every kind
Franks and Franken
and Frankenstein

The one she chose
Ms. Stein it said
the others turned
too many heads

Then to the mall
for skinny jeans
and chocolate treats
for Halloween

⬥ VAMPING AIN'T EASY ⬥

Marcellus Periwhimple
(as told to Thomas I. Benton)

God, I hate those *Twilight* books.

Eternal unlife feeding on pretty girls was bad enough already, what with me wanting to do something other than eat them, but that was before they decided vampires are uber-sexy and kind of sparkly. Now every girl I want to snack on wants me in her sack, so my existence has found whole new levels of agony.

Look, I don't want to be all crude here, but you, umm, know how it is that, uh, a man ... functions, right? A guy needs blood to get it up, and if he can't get it up, well, he can't get it on. Oh, sure, a dude without the blood of life in him can make out all night long, but he can't actually do the final deed. That really blows. I'm here to tell you, lots of girls find *that* inconvenience even hotter, and less threatening, than a fully functioning fellow. Lots of them want to fix me. They get all excited to be that special first one for me. At least until I bite them.

Look, don't hate me, what else am I supposed to do? A vamp has to eat. Besides, no matter how good my intentions are, after all of the teasing and coy giggles, I just can't take it anymore. The only satisfaction I can take is in the warmth of their necks. Other warmths are forever denied me.

The worst of it all is that I got myself vamped *just* when I thought I was going to lose my virginity. She seemed like such a nice girl when I met her at what kids those days called a cotillion. She had flowing red hair, green eyes, and a dress that fit her figure just like a girl from one of those dreams I'd been having, the dreams that had my mother calling both the priest and the doctor. She kept coming back to me every few songs, and I didn't mind one bit. When my favorite dance partner of the night suggested that we slip away to be alone in the dark night, she seemed a lot less nice to me, but a hell of a lot more interesting. We snuck out of the party and down a dark alley. I had already undone her bodice with one hand and my breeches with the other, all while she was nibbling on my neck.

Then she did more than nibble. There I was, all primed for my first bit of carnal knowledge, and the next thing I knew, I was one of the undead—but still without any carnal knowledge.

The worst part was, even though the life blood that I needed to do the deed was sucked right out of me, the *desire* didn't go away with my ability to perform. The lady vampires tell me that they can still get intimate with a mortal, it just doesn't feel the same, is all. Us gentlemen vamps don't even have that option. I wish the red-haired vixen that made me had at least done me that one favor before bringing me through to the other side, but no. Now I am stuck with my V-card forever.

I wish that I could say that I'm not bitter, but I'm bitter as all hell. Sure, there're lots of great things about being on this side. The super-strength is fun. The near infinite unlifespan is at least handy, since dying is now one less thing to worry about. My magical abilities are darn useful. I know things about both the World of Life and the World Beyond that no mortal man can understand. The knowledge that I want most, though, the *real* knowledge of life, that's forever denied me.

I never did like my situation of eternal titillation, but for a couple of centuries there I was able to take comfort in the way girls ran screaming when they learned what I am. That way, there wasn't this layer of temptation impossible for me to satisfy, I just held them down and made a nice meal of them. Now, though, I tell a girl what I am, and she'll get all dewy-eyed and start to get cozy with me. They're always all, "Oh, I understand," and "You poor thing," and "Let me help you" as they put their warm hands on me, the breath of their words warming my cold ears. It's terrible.

Sure, meals are easier this way, but everything else is worse. What good is it if I can get to her neck, but I can't do what I want

with the rest of her? It's no good, no good at all.
   I blame that bitch Stephenie Meyer.

⬥ CELL #666 ⬥

Julia Burton

certifiably insane
he paces his 10 x 10 padded domain
listening to voices only he can hear
screaming out his rage and fear
voices that tell him how to kill
but he is denied his murderous thrill
he gazes out through bars of steel
remembering how it used to feel
when he performed his secret deeds
feeding his maniacal needs
he started at an early age
killing his pets in their cage
but he always wanted more
that is when he went next door
it was on the morning news
how they tracked his bloody shoes
he was found asleep in his bed
clutched to his chest—her severed head

he was such a wonderful son
teaching him to murder was so much fun
but now he's in a padded cell
and my secrets—he'll never tell
I am already teaching son #2—
he will be better than his big brother when I am through

◆ FIVE KISSES ◆

Terry Durbin

In Whitechapel's alleys did Red Jack lurk
awaiting the moment for his blade's cold work.
Throughout the autumn of eighty-eight
five young women met a ghastly fate.
A kiss on the throat from the Ripper's knife
and each lady fell, drained of her life.
But Jack's twisted chore was far from finished
as his need for blood was hardly diminished.
The things he did made London weep,
kidneys, and wombs, and a heart did he keep.
Then into the fog he disappeared like a thought,
to watch and to revel in the fear he'd wrought.
What became of Jack no one can say,
some say he's out there, even today.

◆ STILL LIFE ◆

Joshua Slone

Quentin had never seen a dead body before. Not really. Sure, he'd gone to funerals and glanced in passing at the ninety-year-olds decorated in their coffins, all painted up and manicured, beset by flowers and old photographs, but that was status quo—expected, unexceptional. He'd perused a few pictures of corpses on some internet shock sites when he was a teenager, but this was different. Now, he watched with curiosity as the young lady in front of him writhed and panicked, her pleas for help muffled by the duct tape across her mouth. He watched her thin, frantic hands struggle against their zip-tie restraints behind her back, and he pitied her. She had to know it was just a matter of time now. Her blood-smeared torso bounced from side to side as she wrestled to push herself up off of the concrete floor. Her movements weakened and slowed with each desperate second until they had ceased completely.

Twenty minutes had passed since his victim had settled into her final pose and still Quentin hadn't moved. He studied her like artwork, admired the brushstrokes of her body through the pooled blood coagulating on the floor in front of him. He found her beautiful—perfect, even. He read poetry in the rough contortion of her limbs and exhaled with pleasure at the sight of her.

The product of his endeavor amazed him even more than he'd expected. Her name was Lillian. He snapped a few deliberate photographs, finally moving from his seat in preparation for the task of cleaning up.

If it were up to him, she would lay there forever. She looked so graceful, so surreal. He sighed at the thought of destroying such beauty as he dragged her limp body across the smooth pavement floor of his studio, her bloody wake a sort of signature in his mind. He traced the contours of her still-warm body one last time, as he loaded her remains into his ceramics kiln. Once finished, he fired up the oven and made his way across the studio to the bare mattress and thin sheet strewn out on the opposite side of the room.

He reclined in leisure and lit a cigarette. Somewhere in the deep blue hue of the nighttime skyline outside his studio window, he knew he should feel remorse—if not for Lillian, then for himself. He knew, at some basic level, he should feel worried or anxious; like he should catch the first flight out of the state, seek out some new identity a hundred miles away in quiet anonymity. He knew this, but he didn't run. Somehow, everything just felt right for the moment. Like destiny. Like prophecy.

He ran his fingers through the smoke above him the same as he had her hair earlier. He could still smell the faint evidence of her on his pillowcase—could still taste her on his lips. He'd meant it when he'd called her beautiful and could tell that she'd taken refuge in his flattery. Whatever misery she was attempting to drown in his arms that night had her running in all directions. She felt alone and uncertain in life, she had admitted to him in the afterglow of their evening, the alcohol on her breath guiding the words. He held her gently, coaxed her into sleep. She made mention of how fast his heart was beating as she closed her eyes and nodded off.

An hour later, Quentin drifted into sleep, dreaming of bright futures and wide freedom, the scent of scorching flesh lingering throughout the quiet air which surrounded him. Tomorrow would be a new day, he'd reckoned as he'd laid down to rest. There would be plenty of time to clean the floor and grind up the bones in the morning. Missing persons cases attracted little attention in the city until forty-eight hours or so had passed. By then, Lillian would be a pile of ash in a coffee can. Hell, he might even have her scattered at the base of some Sequoia in the Sierra Nevada by that time. He remembered her saying she had always wanted to visit the park and see those giant trees for herself. She had trusted him with that information. The least he could do now was see to it that she made it out there after her long trek westward from Virginia.

◈ MEMOIRS OF A VAMPIRE SLAYER ◈

Julia Burton

Stakes and holy water you will find
in any good vampire slayer's kit—
these tools are essential—
or else he will get bit.

He also carries a mirror
and cloves of garlic, too.
Once he finds the bloodthirsty creep,
he knows just what to do.

He tracks the vamp creature,
skulking in its casket deep,
he hammers a stake through its heart
as it lies in undead sleep.

The vampire's eyes pop open
as it screams in mortal fear,
from its ancient orbs there falls
a single bloody tear.

The slayer's job is finished,
he packs his tools when he's done,
and thinks it such a pity,
because killing vampires is so much fun.

◆ A TERRIBLE RACE ◆

Terry Durbin

I picked a trail, not my usual path,
And now I fear the demon's wrath.

Branches clutch and thorns they tear
As I run the gauntlet of the woods I fear.

I hear it there, keeping pace,
Biding its time in this terrible race.

I run, I bleed, with one thought in mind,
'Tis the edge of the forest I must find!

Dawn's light could save me from the savaging beast
But it gains from the west as I flee east.

Its stench surrounds me sapping my will,
But lo there ahead is the top of the hill!

The mount's crest marks the edge of the brush,
So it is there I must flee—faster I rush.

I have found the path, so I redouble my pace,
A hopeful smile crossing my face.

I've beaten the beast, its sound no more behind.

Rose twilight ahead, victory is mine!

But what's this looming before me, blocking my trail?
'Tis the demon-thing laughing and saying, "You fail!"

◆ DEAR ZOMBIE GENERAL ◆

Kyle Richardson

Dear Zombie General,

I am writing to you on behalf of the human survivors. We are tired of fighting. We wish to find a peaceful means to coexist. I hope we can work together to achieve this end in some way.

Please let me know how we can accomplish this.

Sincerely,

Captain Reginald Orben

◆ ◆ ◆

deEr humen kaptin,

wee wannt tto eEt yoo branez.

taNk yoo hmm?

zombY genrall

◆ ◆ ◆

Dear Zombie General,

It has come to my attention that my previous attempt to reach a treaty has failed. Last night, a dozen of your troops attacked our fort. We lost two good men. Benny had a wife and three young children. Alfred was only nineteen.

All your invading soldiers have been incapacitated. Their remains will be burned. You will see the smoke on the horizon.

Please, I am asking, from one leader to another, let us end this violence and find a means for peace.

Hopefully,

Captain Reginald Orben

◆ ◆ ◆

der hUmin,

wee sen moar ov uss too eet yoO branez.

wy yoo keeEp riting mee? ai noh gUd att riteeng. tokiNg betar.

yoo welKum mhmm,

zOmby genrall

◆ ◆ ◆

Dear Zombie General,

It appears you will not be bargained with. We have full military capabilities. Our ammunition stockpile is more than adequate to neutralize any threat your ground troops may pose.

In the interest of preserving the chance for a future cure, I ask that you order your troops to stand down at once.

Adamantly,

Captain Reginald Orben

❖ ❖ ❖

deer heEyoomen,

wee zomBys doo naht wahnt too dai. wee zombys skared, juS lyk heeyoomins.

pleez tok too mEe. noh faiTing. zomby too heeyoOmin. wee toK. wee shEik hanz. ai doo naHt eet yoo, wee promeEs. yoo doo nAht chute me, yoo promees. wee fyNd solushin. wee fynd peEce.

yess nOh okey,

zoMby genralL

❖ ❖ ❖

Dear Zombie General,

I am pleased to receive your reasonable response, and I will honor your request to meet.

I will be accompanied by armed guards. Please do not be offended by this. I consider it a necessary precaution.

I hope we will soon be shaking hands and moving toward a brighter, more prosperous future.

Gratefully,

Captain Reginald Orben

❖ ❖ ❖

deer heeyOomins,

wee eeTed yur kaptins branez. wee eeted yUr gards branez. dEy tazted veree gud.

pleez kuM tok too uss. wee feLl badd. wee wahnt too apOleejize. pleez kuM wid meny ov yoo.

okie haY hii,

zOmby genRall

◈ MALIGNANT DESIRES ◈

Julia Burton

Centuries come
and centuries go
as my malignant
powers grow.

Soon I'll be
released from my tomb.
You mortals will taste
of your terrible doom.

I will tear small
bones asunder
as your children
I plunder.

And, oh yes,
I have a name—
the Beast and I
were born the same.

◆ SOMETHING WICKED ◆

T. Kent

Something wicked gives me death
Turns me into a rotting shell
Then kisses purple lips with breath
Returns my life with earth my hell

Something wicked seethes inside
Permeates bones and veins and skin
Evil heart and deadened eyes
Thoughts of pain and death and sin

Something wicked comes your way
Fear me now, for I am vile
Hide your soul, get far away
I'll share my fate with a hellish smile

◆ ZOMBIES RISING ◆

Julia Burton

Advancing army of zombies
Rising from moss covered tombs
Restless filthy creatures
Moving in the purple gloom
Rattling bones and rotting rags
Macabre mindless grins
Nightmare army of destruction
Of children, women, and men
Grasping bony fingers
Staggering lurching gait
Following the alluring scent
Of living human bait

❖ THE COLLECTOR ❖

Terry Durbin

"You said you are a collector."

He heard the woman's voice, but only in the way you sometimes hear voices coming from a television in another room. He was looking at the children. Oh! The glorious children. Ten of them. The same number he had at home. Ten children lined up in this cellar room, five to a side, as if preparing to play Red Rover.

"Do you have anything like this?" Her tone was smug.

"Yes," he said. "And no." He placed the plastic bag containing the photograph and figurine he'd purchased in the shop upstairs on the floor at the feet of the first child. He could see the Nike swoosh embossed onto the cream-colored sneakers on her cream-colored feet.

"Isn't she pretty?" The woman stood at the base of the stairs leading up to the shop. Her gray dress blended like camouflage with the concrete block wall behind her.

"She is," he admitted. "She looks…" He almost said 'like Audriana.' He needed to be careful. It wouldn't do to say that name. *No worry*, he thought. *You're always careful. You wouldn't have your collection if you weren't.*

But she did look like Audriana, or, at least what Audriana had looked like before the salt and formaldehyde. She looked like what he remembered. Audriana was, after all, his first.

"What are they made of?" His fingers brushed lightly over the smooth, almost featureless face under Audriana's curls. "Plaster?"

"Papier-mâché."

"Of course." Now that she'd told him, he saw the unmistakable texture of the fibers in the girl's closed eyelids and on her perfect cheeks. "Remarkable." The face was only vaguely rendered; just a hint of full lips, a rumor of a nose, but the clothes were sculpted with exacting detail. "Remarkable."

He moved to the next life-sized simulacrum. A boy with long, straight hair and a Dallas Cowboys jacket. He brushed Ethan's fingertips with his own. A pain lanced through the pad of his ring finger.

"Oww!" He jerked back his hand and sucked away a swelling trickle of blood. The coppery taste of it thrilled him.

"The paper isn't as soft as it looks," the woman said. "There's something in it that makes it mean."

What a strange way to put it, he thought. *Children are never mean.* He stepped across the narrow aisle separating the files of paper children. Gordon... Dakota... Cassie... Naturally they couldn't really be sculptures of his children. His children were hidden. Safe. He'd been so careful. And his children had eyes, and faces.

Saying nothing, he continued down the row: Misty with her jump rope... Charlotte's plump arms... Ian's ball cap turned backward... Connor... Tammy... But, of course... not. At the end of the papier-mâché gauntlet was another cement block wall. He turned and looked back. The old, incandescent lights overhead cast black slashes of shadow over his children. The merciless light tricked his eyes. Where before, the vague, nearly featureless faces had been staring straight ahead like paper dolls, now they seemed to be turned toward him like silent students in an underground classroom. *My children*, he thought. *See how they love me?*

"How much do you want for them?"

The woman still stood at the base of the stairs. She smiled and shook her head slowly. "It's not what I want for them," she said, in her soft, smoky voice. "It's what they want from you."

He felt his face flush. He stepped forward. Tammy was on his right—she was his newest—Connor on his left. "I have no idea what you are..."

"That's right," she interrupted. "You have no idea at all."

In perfect synchronicity, ten pair of paper eyelids opened onto twenty eyeless sockets filled with a living seething blackness, like twenty doors into the same hell.

With a quiet 'click' the lights went out. In the absolute darkness paper rustled.

⬥ JUST BEYOND ⬥

Joshua Slone

From the hurried world,
I disengage,
the winter air sent
slowly whirling,
all cool and sharp
and dead,
shakes me out
of warm reality,
lays me down into
the open earth,
whisks me through
the grave, into austere
white oblivion, full of questions
acknowledged by
the gentle gloaming's silence,
punctuated with quick, hot breaths
offered like a sacrifice
to Time.

With busy minds
and shining eyes
fixed desperate to
the light on the horizon,
it's no wonder
we rarely notice
that great chasm
just beyond.

◆ DIRGE OF THE DEAD ◆

Julia Burton

In gothic spires beyond iron gates
silent bells patiently wait
to ring a dirge of grief and doom
for those sleeping in the tombs.
Behind the mausoleum wall
waiting for night to fall,
they murmur in uneasy sleep
disturbed by the tears you weep.
So take your cloying sweet bouquet
and do not return 'til the light of day.

◈ COUNTRY RUFFIANS ◈

Tom Benton

When I was born, my parents' house didn't have an indoor toilet. That situation didn't last long. My great-grandparents couldn't stand to think of me, not only their first great-grandchild, but also the first born son of the first born son of their first born son, being left alone while my mother went outside to answer nature's call. My great-grandparents paid to plumb the house before I was big enough to even crawl. So, when I was growing up our outhouse was a mere novelty to me, just a smaller and slightly more decrepit shack behind the larger and less decrepit shack we lived in.

Outhouses were no mere novelty to my great-grandpa.

Every October, Gramps would tell me about tricks a group of hillbillies called the 'country ruffians' used to play in town on Halloween night, back when he was young. He never quite admitted to having been one of the country ruffians, but then he never explained how he could have had such intimate knowledge of the hillbilly Halloween mayhem they caused without being one of the group.

He told me how the ruffians would come in from the farms around town for Halloween socializing. As there were very few treats to be had in those days, the ruffians focused on the tricks. Back then, even folks who lived in town didn't have indoor plumbing. The ruffians discovered they could sneak along from backyard to backyard just after dusk, picking up each outhouse and moving it back a few feet further from the big house. Then those young men would sit in the dark waiting to hear the hollers of folks who fell into their outhouse pit when they went to take their evening constitutional by the light of a kerosene lantern.

Old Man Moore gave the country ruffians their name. He was their chief target and most violent opponent. He sounded like the sort of man even a quartet of liquored up farm boys would have feared when he was just a bit younger. Back when the ruffians were busy moving the town's privies, Moore was a mountain of a man with a dignified white mane, still physically intimidating but rapidly losing his race with Father Time.

Every year after the first latrine trick, Old Man Moore would try to guard his outhouse from the country ruffians with a dog and a gun, but the only effect was to make the target all the more appealing. With craftiness in the darkness, the ruffians would move Moore's outhouse every year. Sometimes they had to wait until early morning, but eventually he would climb out of the stinking hole bellowing like an angry bull while the boys laughed and called him a 'shit baby.' The ruffians would stop laughing and run off down the dirt street when Moore started firing off rounds with his old shotgun.

As the years wore on and the country ruffians got older, they became more interested in women and whiskey than in playing tricks with privies, but Old Man Moore's outhouse still held a special place in their hearts. So for one last time they met up in town for some fun at Old Man Moore's expense. While the sun was still up they'd got liquored up good and promised some young townswomen a visit later in the evening. With bellies full of whiskey and dreams of a night with a girl apiece, the ruffians settled in behind Old Man Moore's back fence to await their chance.

In the last bit of daylight they could see Old Man Moore's white shock of hair moving to and fro above his rocking chair on the back porch. They could just make out the dark barrel of the shotgun against his long white beard as Moore cradled the gun in his lap. The old hound dog that had chased the young men for so many times before was nowhere to be seen. The ruffians could barely contain their giggles when they saw that the old man was already starting to nod off in the failing light.

Once it got good and dark, and they could hear dramatic snores coming from the direction of the porch, the young men thought of the women who were waiting for them and decided it was time to get the show on the road. One by one, they slithered under the planks of the fence, taking care to keep the smaller darkness of the outhouse between them and the larger darkness of Old Man Moore's house. The ruffians crept along through the tall grass between the fence and the outhouse as stealthily as four farm boys could, planning on reaching the back of the privy and then slinking along the walls to each take a corner to lift it back a few feet.

They screamed something terrible when the ground gave way beneath them. The outhouse suddenly loomed higher above them than before, and then they were flailing off of one another in a pit filled with a foul smelling slurry.

Laughter boomed from the porch on the other side of the outhouse. "You goddam ruffians ain't the only ones can move a privy! How do youins like being shit babies now?" The ruffians scrambled at the edge of the pit, but they got serious about running when they heard Old Man Moore open his backdoor and yell, "Sic 'em, Bo!" Then the gun boomed along with Moore's laughter.

Gramps never told me how he knew so much about the antics of the country ruffians, but he did tell me that you never realize how fast you can run until you're mixing your own shit with someone else's as the someone else sends both a hunting dog and shotgun blasts after you.

He also told me that he hated not getting to meet up with that girl later.

◆ RUNNING SCARED ◆

Julia Burton

in the dark
it hides and waits
when you pass by
don't hesitate

please don't scream
please don't cry
you can't get away
don't even try

run and jump
into your bed
pull the covers
over your head

what is that sound
the floorboards creak
and bony fingers
caress your cheek

IT followed you home
right to your room
It's hiding there
crouched in the gloom

◈ DEAR MARY ◈

Terry Durbin

Dear Mary,

I know that you love me and that you are just shy.
I know it because of the look in your eye.
When I saw you on campus you smiled and said "Hi!"
Your love was implied; I'm a sensitive guy.

So I wrote you a letter expressing my love,
But you never replied, you shy, shy dove.
So I called just to hear you like an angel from above.

I followed and I watched both by day and by night,
Your protector forever always just out of sight.

Till that night at your window when you saw and screamed "Help!"

The cops came and told me to stay away from your street.
I know you didn't want it and I swore we would meet.

I must possess you, it's destined to be,
Forever together just you and me.
A love like ours as enduring as the sea.

From your closet I came with a stealthy lover's grace.

My future was sealed by the look on your face.
Our eternity starts now, in this candle-lit space,
Forever entwined in your cold, dead embrace.

Yours Forever

◈ THE PERFECT MATCH ◈

T. Kent

I've been watching my husband have sex with other women.

I know—sounds kinky. But before you judge too harshly, let me explain.

After ten years of marriage, we'd become 'Byron and Elise,' the poster couple for toxic relationships.

Our love had turned *ugly*—criticism and sarcasm the only language we understood.

Public snark attacks were the worst. All it took was for someone to ask, "How long have you two been together?" and we'd be on a roll.

I'd say, "Ten years."

Byron would say, "Yeah, two of the best years of my life."

Then I'd say, "And he's got me beat by a year."

We were miserable—but neither of us was leaving.

Byron stayed because he coveted the spoils of my trust fund. He'd grown up in a sad little white-trash trailer park in South Georgia and wasn't about to give up the Tudor-style brick home overlooking the golf course, the three-car garage with matching 328is and a Range Rover Sport, the trips to Aruba and Paris.

I stayed because I coveted Byron. He was the perfect trophy husband—Jerry Seinfield funny, George Clooney gorgeous, and when he wanted to be, a lover right out of the pages of my trashy romance novels.

The crazy thing was, despite my participation in our mutual animosity society, I still loved him and wanted us to be happy again. And I knew that deep down Byron loved me too. If I could just get him to tap into those feelings, I was sure I could save our marriage.

What I needed was a plan—something *big* to jolt him to his senses. They say you don't know what you've got until it's gone. Byron needed to *think* I was gone.

So I spent weeks crafting a sentimental, conciliatory goodbye note. I reminded him of the sheet-clenching, toe-curling, panty-melting sex we used to have, the days we played hooky from work to go to the zoo or the museum, the way we always had each other's back when his deadbeat dad, my overbearing parents, or the world in general threatened our utopia.

It was the perfect note for the perfect faux suicide.

On a sunny Wednesday, when I knew Byron was coming straight home from work to change for tennis, I put my plan into action. I took a few sleeping pills and flushed the rest of the bottle down the toilet, drank a glass of bourbon, and put on my sexiest Agent Provocateur lingerie. Then I lay down and slept.

I misjudged two things that day: the amount of pills and alcohol it would take to kill me and what Byron would do when he found me. I never *dreamed* the son-of-a-bitch would leave me there to die.

I knew he was an asshole. But a murderer? *Seriously*?

Fortunately, one door never closes without another one opening, and as I watched my husband whistle a merry tune while primping for my funeral a few days later, it hit me. I was dead—but I wasn't gone!

I did a ghostly imitation of a happy dance with one thought in mind.

Game on.

There was no instruction manual for becoming a ghost, so I learned the ropes through trial and error. By the time Byron started bringing women home three months later, I knew a few things. Like the fact that I couldn't leave the bedroom where I'd died, and the fact that I drew my power from the energy of humans. I also had a few ghostly tools at my disposal, but I could only use them when my strength was at its peak.

That's when I started watching Byron have sex—because a ghost can draw a lot of energy from two sweaty humans going at it like animals. At the point of climax, I'd feel an amazing jolt of static electricity ripple through me, and *that's* when I could do things.

Did I enjoy watching my husband with other women? Hell no. It made me crazy with jealousy. But it was a means to an end, a way to even the score. Not that the score could ever be evened. I was dead. He was not. But I did take some amount of comfort in shaking up his little world. He may have won the war, but I was like a pocket of resistant rebels—I was winning the skirmishes.

My favorite pastime? Scaring off the bitches he brought home.

Like the model, Alexis—tall, dark, and high maintenance. An only child and a whiner.

"Byron, why don't you take me out more often? Why don't you sell this house?" (Uh, because it's not his, bimbo, it belongs to my trust.)

Alexis even whined during sex. I'm not kidding. The worst punishment would have been to let him keep her, but I had no patience for the long game. All it took was one look at my shimmering apparition over Byron's left shoulder when he was pumping her full of his love juice, and she was out of here.

Then there was Rebecca—voluptuous, redheaded Rebecca. That was the day I realized that if I focused all my energy on Byron, I could fill his head with my image. Timing was everything. Rebecca wasn't too happy at the moment of truth to hear him yell, "Oh God… Eliiise." Never saw Red again.

The last one was Evelyn. When he showed up with her, I'd just figured out how to make my trademark fragrance—Juicy Couture—permeate the bedroom. They were pretty hot and heavy when she smelled it and thought he'd been cheating. We'll miss you Evelyn. *Not*.

There hadn't been any other girls for a month, but Byron was bringing someone home tonight. He'd put on his black briefs this morning. That was a sure sign.

But something happened that had me on edge. I was hovering at the open bathroom door, watching him towel off from his shower (I still enjoyed seeing him naked—so sue me). Anyway, he stepped over to the steamy mirror and wrote *Elise, I've got a surprise for you tonight* with his finger. Then he wiped it off slowly with a towel and smiled so big his cheeks were probably still hurting.

What. The. Hell. Byron was obviously in on my game.

I'd been rippling with anxiety all day.

He came home at around eight with company. From downstairs, I heard their laughter intermingle with a Prince song from *our* old 'Date Night' playlist. *Grrrrr.*

An hour later the bedroom door finally opened, and he ushered his new girl in.

This one had long black hair and dark-rimmed glasses. She looked like a schoolteacher—a sexy, beautiful schoolteacher. I hated her instantly.

Byron stopped inside the door and pulled her close, kissing her deeply.

Oh, jealousy is a crazy mistress. I was foot-stomping, plate-throwing mad, but couldn't do a damn thing about it. *Enjoy it while it lasts buddy.*

I watched as he walked her backwards to the bed and pushed gently so that she sat down with a bounce. He grabbed a wrapped gift box from a dresser drawer and brought it to her.

"For me? What's this for?" she asked in a gaggingly sweet voice.

"Just for being you. Go ahead, open it." He sat down next to her on the bed and placed his arm across her shoulders.

She tore into the paper and squealed, "Juicy Couture. Oh, I *love* this fragrance."

Juicy-Fucking-Couture. That was *my* fragrance, not hers. I felt my essence tremble as she sprayed a liberal amount on each of her wrists, then a final shot down the front of her dress. She giggled when Byron leaned over and rubbed his nose in her cleavage.

"Here let me take this off of you." Byron slowly lifted her dress over her head and tossed it on a chair in the corner. Then he pulled her glasses off and set them on the side table.

"Byron, wait. You know I can't see two feet in front of me without my glasses."

He held her head tenderly between both hands and kissed her again. "Everything you need to see in this room is right in front of you."

I was fuming. But that was fine. When the time was right, I was going to sear myself into his brain. He'd scream *Elise* so loud it would wake up the neighborhood. Let's see how schoolteacher liked that.

Byron removed the rest of her clothes and then his own. He scooted himself back on the bed and pulled her onto his lap, facing him. I could see his face plainly over her shoulder when he said to her, "Elise, what a pretty name. I think you're the perfect match for me." Then he looked at me and winked. I'm absolutely sure of it.

The half-blind, Juicy Couture-wearing bitch named Elise giggled again.

That. Dirty. Bastard.

◆ INSIDE MY HEAD ◆

Terry Durbin

Inside my head it is crowded.
It is crowded inside my head.
Too many voices whispering,
voices suggesting who should be dead.
I walk next to you in the market,
and watch you shower from behind the shed.
I touched your hair once in a crowded theater,
and now I wonder just where to put your head.
Can I tell you that I love you,
or would you run if that was said?
If you listen I promise to make you smile,
I can do it with wires and needles and thread.

◆ UNDER THE COVERS ◆

T. Kent

Tell me how you fear the dark
I'll find the source and steal your light

Tell me how you jump at sounds
I'll fill the air with howls each night

Tell me spirits make you shake
I'll haunt the halls inside your head

Tell me monsters make you cry
I'll make my home beneath your bed

◆ BLOODMOON ARIA ◆

Julia Burton

Usher in this bloodmoon night,
as the vermilion moon takes flight.
Alien creatures begin to roam
and exotic birds sing an ancient song,
the purple abyss opens in the ground
responding to the bewitching sound,
as all creatures start to sing
of the rapture the bloodmoon brings.

The aria turns to an anguished wail
as the waning moon turns pale.
Now they sing a desolate tune,
mourning the death of the crimson moon.

⟡ OF RITUAL ⟡

Joshua Slone

"N'ghut virax ez miora hiltemk," Franklin chanted from the motel bathroom. The linoleum flooring had been torn away revealing the cold concrete beneath it. He sat cross-legged and naked at the center of a chalk pentagram littered on all sides with hastily scribbled incantations. The lady lying on the bed in his room feigned post-coital moans of ecstasy punctuated by a hacking cough. He repeated his chant, clasping a small piece of rough-hewn onyx in his hands, his body glistening with sweat.

The room smelled like sex and mildew. The smoke from his companion's cigarette drew soft, grey kaleidoscope patterns in the air. "The fuck you doin' in there, anyways?" she asked, draped across the mattress like the subject of an oil painting. She pulled the dingy sheet up over one shoulder, leaving a single, small breast drooping from her makeshift cocoon. "You only paid for two hours, ya know?" she exhaled a plume of smoke, the words trailing out behind. "Your dime, though. Clock's tickin'."

Franklin rocked back and forth, his body turned away from her, muttering incoherently, desperate. The smooth angles of the stone clenched in his fist broke the skin. A trickle of blood traced the side of his palm and wrist. He felt sharp, stabbing pains jab throughout his abdomen; watched the quick, defined shapes protruding from his belly at random. He shut his eyes tight and gritted his teeth, still uttering his recitation, "N'ghut virax ez miora hiltemk."

The woman rolled onto her back, hanging her head upside-down over the edge of bed. She moaned with scripted pleasure, "Why don'chya come on back to bed, sweetie? I'm gettin' cold. Come on over and warm me up." Franklin ignored the suggestion, instead continuing his quick rocking and hushed rambling. She flopped onto her stomach, propped herself up on her elbows. "Look, man. I don't know what the hell all this weird ass shit is about, but you got twenty minutes or two-hundred more bucks 'til I'm gone." She took one last drag off her cigarette before stamping it out in an aluminum ashtray on the floor.

As she bent down to retrieve the ashtray, she noticed a line of what appeared to be salt on the carpet. "The fuck?" She remembered Franklin pacing around the room right after their brief intercourse, but she'd been too busy fumbling through her purse looking for her Camels to notice what he was doing. She followed it around the bed, noticed it stopping fast against the wall on either side. She laughed out loud, condescending of his apparent fetish. "Ha ha! You get off on some strange shit, huh?" She hoisted herself back up to the head of the bed still cloaked in the stiff, yellowed bed sheet. "I ain't complainin' 'bout easy money or nothin', but if we're done here, I wanna shower whenever you're finished in there."

"N'ghut virax ez miora hilte..." the room stuttered and shook, the lights flickered, almost rattling off the walls and ceiling. Franklin ceased his invocation, turned to face the woman as she shot up in the bed, her head swinging from side to side.

The bed sheet fell to her waist as she planted her hands firm against the mattress on either side. "What the hell's goin' on?" she asked in disbelief. She covered her face in her arms as a mirror clattered from the wall to the floor, shattering against the ground. She lunged toward the edge of the bed but stopped abruptly, inches from the salt barrier. She gasped, choking on her own breath, clutching her hands to her throat as bile and blood seeped out from the corners of her mouth. Her eyes bulged, tears streaking through the sloppy rouge on her cheeks. She struggled to scream as the slimy, black tendrils slithered past her lips, writhing like earthworms in wet soil. With each flailing inch, the creature lurched out from deep inside its new host as the woman's face, throat and torso slowly ripped apart from its bulk. One final thrust split her fully in half down to her legs as the creature sprawled out its wide body, its screeching cry bouncing off the blood-splattered walls.

Franklin fell back against the bathroom door, panting and relieved. He ran his hands up and down his stomach, wrapped his arms tight around himself. "There. You happy?" he finally managed, pulling himself up off the floor by the doorknob. The creature slithered from one side of the bed to the other letting out a guttural roar, corralled within its salt-circle prison. "Oh no," Franklin huffed between labored breaths, a serrated grin carved across his face, "we're not done here." He stumbled toward the thing on the bed, stopping a few inches away from the white line on the floor. "Now, I need you to do something for me."

◆ THE OLD ONES ◆

Terry Durbin

Remember you this, oh arrogant mortals, that we are the Old Ones who built all the portals,
which let us roam throughout your nights, bringing with us a darkness to defeat all your lights.

So, believe if you must in logic and science, but know in your dreams it's a hollow defiance.

For your pride and your hubris come with a cost:
You are really quite chewy and taste good with sauce.

◆ EVIL SECRETS ◆

Julia Burton

Impossible for the mind to believe
the evil that human monsters can achieve.
Like John Wayne Gacy, as we all know
was the star in his very own horror show.
He played a friendly clown by day
while murdering young men he enslaved.
Thirty-three bodies in shallow graves—
under his house they all were laid.
Neighbors were all sick with fear
to learn a monster lived so near.
We have neighbors on all sides—
ever wonder what secrets they may hide?

ROCKJUNKIE@TWITTER

Terry Durbin

@Rockjunkie: *Heading to Iceland tomorrow!!! Hverfjall volcano and the midnight Sun! Woot! Follow all my thesis project tweets here on Twitter.*

@Rockjunkie: *In Iceland and loving it! 1st activity @ Hverfjall in 900 years! Reykjavik to volcano = long ride, going 2 sleep.*

@Rockjunkie: *Arrived @ Hverfjall 2AM. Still light out! Glow from crater EZ 2 see. Still 20 miles from caldera; sky looks 2B on fire. No smoke/ash - odd.*

@Rockjunkie: *Hverfjall for 2 days now. Mountain doesn't look like much, low, gentle slope. Villagers call it a sleeping dragon, I can see that.*

@Rockjunkie: *24 Hour days freak me out! B-rhythms screwed, can't sleep. People R cool, beer is good, food not. Nice bar in village, love the stories!*

@Rockjunkie: *Spent day placing monitors and taking pics. Lugged everything myself; locals won't go near Hverfjall. Damned superstition!*

@Rockjunkie: *Getting use 2 the smell of rotten eggs, yuck! Eruption growing; seeing long-period quakes @ mag 3. Sky getting brighter above caldera.*

@Rockjunkie: *Village people (YMCA!) R cool. Not 2 backward. 1 Dude (Galdur) even has a Twitter account! Still won't come near mountain.*

@Rockjunkie: *Can you BELIEVE it? Village council wants me 2 pack-up and go! Nice about it, but seemed scared. Can't go. Need this 4 my thesis.*

@Rockjunkie: *Midnight - deep blue sky in south; Sun teasing the horizon north. Burning glow over vent; orange fire where the dragon lives (cool story!).*

@Rockjunkie: *So much for biologists! Books said no reptiles in Iceland. I just killed an ugly-ass snake in my tent. 3ft long. Sick-green. Nasty fangs.*

@Rockjunkie: *Totally weird! Took snake 2 bar and everyone crapped themselves. 1 Old lady threw salt at me! Quakes @ mag 3.7. Something's moving 4 sure.*

@Rockjunkie: *Need 2 move camp. Came back from monitor check 2 find tent tagged like an LA underpass. Symbols everywhere. Not paint—blood.*

@Rockjunkie: *Old lady watched as I washed tent B4 move. Kept yelling, "No no no, save you!" Crazy bitch! Moved camp 2km E, near stream; lots of frogs.*

@Rockjunkie: *Something wrong with monitors. Gas levels FUBAR. CO2, SO2, H2S, all normal? Sulfur smell EVERYWHERE! Quakes have leveled @ mag 3.9.*

@Rockjunkie: *Took hand monitor up flank 2 check gasses, all normal there 2? Smells like rotting meat up high. 2 more snakes @ camp. Creepy!*

@Rockjunkie: *8 Lunch @ 1AM under a smoke-free sky. Saw a flock of birds fly close 2 vent and get fried by yellow flames.*

Nothing like it! Need sleep.

@Rockjunkie: *Damned frogs! Washing up in creek after bkfast and got bit! What kind of frog bites?! Hurts like hell. Squashed its ass. Hundreds more.*

@Rockjunkie: *Finally slept while the ground kept shaking. Dreamed of snakes, frogs and burning sky. Woke up 2 snakes, frogs, and burning sky. HAHA!*

@Rockjunkie: *Feel like crap. Hand swollen and infected. Nothing in medkit works. Going 2 village 2 look for doc. Now there R white worms everywhere.*

@Rockjunkie: *Village empty! Looks like they left in a hurry. Scared of Hverfjall probably. Nice 2 see houses again, felt kind of normal. Miss them.*

@Rockjunkie: *Would kill 4 a dark night! R there still stars out there? Nothing but death-stink and worms here. Saw a big worm eat a frog?! Go worm!*

@Rockjunkie: *Going 2 top of tuft ring with HD cam. Need 2 see how a volcano erupts without smoke, ash and gas. No magma either! Lots of shitty critters!*

@Rockjunkie: *Swollen arm made packing hard. Hand feels dead, smells like it 2! Gotta get help after trip 2 caldera. Enough data for 10 theses.*

@Rockjunkie: *No volcano! Something else! Filled with red mist— it MOVED! Had an EYE! 2 BIG! Looking @ ME! Mountain filled with crawling things—MOVING THI*

@Rockjunkie: *MOVING THINGS! HUNGRY THINGS! THINGS COMING! COMING!!*

@Rockjunkie: *Nice volcano man is gone. Sorry Galdur can not save. Guardian will sleep now. Stay away, thank you.*

◆ LAST CALL ◆

Terry Durbin

Return we must on this All Saints Day,
to our crypts, and our coffins, and to open graves.
Our 'Spirit Walk' is finished—the dawn you mortals spared.
Another year will we lie beneath the sod, in the dark
While the worms in our eyes do their recycling work.
But, as faithful as death, I promise you this,
Next Halloween night we'll share a rank embrace.

◈ STEWED ◈

Julia Burton

Gentle moon,
star spangled night,
in a drunken state
the witch takes flight.

She grabs her broom,
her cape and hat,
finishes the whiskey
and calls her cat.

Then off they go
into the night,
guided by the
moon's bright light.

She swoops and glides
and laughs in glee—
never has she
felt so free.

Then she screams
"Hey, look at me!"
her final words
before she hits a tree.

⬥ MAYHEM ⬥

Thomas I. Benton

The used books lining the shelves of the spare bedroom told the tale of Abby's marriage. Abby didn't like the story much. It began by the door, with titles like *Finding Fertility*. By the closet the story changed to *Build the Family You Deserve: Making Adoption Work for You*. The chapters under the window bore titles like *Rekindling the Fire: Reclaiming the Passion in Your Marriage*.

Abby sat at the end of the books, hating herself for reading a glossy magazine she had bought at the T&C while she was picking up the extra bags of candy her fool husband insisted he needed for trick-or-treaters. That girl whose name she could never remember from Bob's class a couple years before gave Abby that nasty look at checkout. Maybe she just hated everyone, Abby told herself.

Abby could hear Bob handing out the candy as she thumbed through page after page of advice on handling husbands. The pitch of the voices out front changed, until finally the voices were entirely too old to still be trick-or-treating. Bob insisted that there was nothing wrong with his high school students coming by the house, but Abby still didn't like it. One of them had given him that creepy Guy Fawkes mask that dangled from the doorknob by her knee.

Abby paused when the inspiration hit. She looked at her magazine for a final shot of courage, then rummaged until she found a spare sheet in the closet. She tossed the magazine to the end of her books, grabbed the mask, and climbed through the window as gracefully as she could.

Like the dozens of times before, Abby decided to make one last attempt at saving her marriage. She didn't know why she bothered to work so hard when Bob didn't even seem to care. Then again, she reminded herself, she wasn't getting any younger, and most of the men around were like Bob's no-account brother. Her marriage was worth saving, so she removed her clothes and donned the sheet and mask. Bob was getting a treat for Halloween, whether he wanted it or not.

❖ ❖ ❖

Bob loved Halloween. There was something pure about a child wanting sugar, and he assured himself there was something noble about his enthusiasm for providing the sweetness they craved. Abby never could understand that, but then Abby couldn't understand a lot of things. He thought about the things Abby couldn't understand as he tossed fistfuls of tiny chocolate bars, jelly beans, and candy corn into the sacks held open before him.

Carla had been pressing him about Abby lately. Carla had a point, but the scandal of the most popular teacher in town leaving his wife for a former student would leave him without a job. Keeping his job was the only reason to stay with Abby, but that reason was more than good enough. Bob might have loved Abby once, long ago, before she scheduled their love life according to her basal body temperature. Even the scheduled sex was better than when Abby got a notion to try to fix their love life, though; all the fixes seemed to involve them doing everything but having sex, nothing but talking and walking and other nonsense. There was a lot Abby couldn't understand.

Bob had seen Carla during her work break on his way home after school. Five minutes locked in the storeroom was all they needed, but he stayed for her entire fifteen minute break, because he was just romantic that way. Even with the extra attention, Carla was acting a little weird. Bob put it out of his head and doled out fruit flavored taffy.

All the while, Bob kept a look out for his drunk brother, who caused a scene most Halloweens, and Carla, who could cause a bigger one than David ever could.

❖ ❖ ❖

BEEP. Carla scanned yet another bag of marked down candy. BEEP. BEEP. BEEP.

Carla thought about Bob handing out the candy his bitch wife had bought that afternoon. Carla knew she belonged there with him, laughing together at the little kids in their costumes. She rubbed her own stomach and thought about costumes for babies.

She'd tried to tell Bob on her break. She just couldn't force the words out. The three pregnancy tests from the T&C pharmacy section peeked out of her purse, accusing her. Once her customer had paid for the bags of cheap sugar, Carla decided the time had come. She turned off her light, tossed a magic marker in with her positive tests, and abandoned her post.

She left her clothes in the storeroom, hiding the scrawled "IT'S YOURS" she wrote in marker on her bare waist under her long coat.

❖ ❖ ❖

David was going to hold up the joint; he really was. He had a pistol tucked into the waist of his pants and planned on using it to make that cute checkout girl give him all the cash in her drawer. She was there when he walked into the T&C, but by the time he got back to the front with a case of beer under his arm and the gun ready to draw she had run off.

David never was good at figuring out what to do when things didn't go to plan, so he ran off with the beer to his brother's place, just like always. The gun was heavy in his pants.

❖ ❖ ❖

The radio buzzed again. Evan hated Halloween and the endless calls for kids up to mischief. Police had better things to do than warn kids caught tossing toilet paper into a tree.

"Shoplifting at the T&C," the radio told him in a bored voice of dispatch. Evan started the five minute drive across town. He was just pulling into the grocery store parking lot when the next call came in on the radio. Dispatch's boredom was replaced by urgency.

"ALL UNITS, GUNFIRE AT 123 OAK! ALL UNITS, GUNFIRE AT 123 OAK!"

◆ BY ANY OTHER NAME ◆

Terry Durbin

'H' to 'I' to 'J' then 'K',
The alphabet killer picks victims this way.

Once each year he roams the streets,
Sorting the fates of the people he meets.

First-middle-last the name doesn't matter,
So long as it fits into his pattern.

Amys and Bookmans and Carries and Dons
Ellys and Freds and Goldblums have gone.

So if your name is Hanna, Horace, or Hopper
I'd say that you're fodder for our Halloween chopper.

With All Hallows looming there's not a minute to waste
In getting to the courthouse with all possible haste.

There I would file a change of my name,
To something safer like Zelda, Zeke, or Zane.

◆ A SINISTER PLACE ◆

T. Kent

old crooked oaks
with roots that strangle
gravestones crumbling
leaned at an angle

ghouls and hellhounds
behind the gates
biding their time
as they patiently wait

a sinister place
once the sun has sunk low
a place where a smart man
would know not to go

ABOUT THE AUTHORS

Thomas I. Benton's great-great-great grandfather arrived in a little town in the Ozarks running from a murder charge; he never left. Five generations later, Tom was raised on a farm in that same town. Hillbillies traditionally don't move around much, and the other Bentons are pretty traditional. Tom moved around, though, starting when he left the hills for a fancy college out east. Now Tom lives in the Kansas City area, which is close enough to the Ozarks for an easy visit but far enough away to deter kin who might want to visit him.

Website: www.ThomasIBenton.com
Amazon: www.amazon.com/author/thomasibenton
Twitter: @ThomasIBenton

Julia Burton writes dark poetry and lives in a small town where she teaches glass blowing.

Amazon: www.amazon.com/author/juliaburton

Terry Durbin is a writer of suspense, horror, and other, less classifiable fiction. He's a husband, father, grandfather, and proud caretaker to two remarkable dogs. His books *Chase*, *The Legacy of Aaron Geist*, and his short story collection, *Reflections in a Black Mirror* are available from Amazon.

Amazon: www.amazon.com/author/terrydurbin
Twitter: @durbinterry

T. Kent is a writer of romance, science fiction, and fantasy, and a dabbler in poetry. She is a wife and mother and has two French Bulldogs who cuddle and pass gas and make her cheeks hurt from smiling. She loves tennis, books, computers, camping, and hiking, in no particular order. She shares her time between Atlanta, GA, and Asheville, NC.

Website: www.tkentwrites.com
Amazon: www.amazon.com/author/tkent
Twitter: @tkentwrites
Facebook: www.facebook.com/tkentwrites

Kyle Richardson writes about steam-powered airships, sentient mechanical pets, and ordinary humans doing extraordinary things. He lives in Canada with his swollen-bellied wife, Michelle. They're expecting their first child in June. His fiction is scheduled to appear in several anthologies this year. His debut novel, a rollicking steampunk adventure, is due at the end of spring.

Website: www.KyleRichardsonBooks.com
Amazon: www.amazon.com/author/kylerichardson

Joshua Slone has been called, "One of the greatest writers of this era," by his grandmother, who truly is the sweetest lady anybody could ever hope to meet. He is a dedicated father and husband and has had a true love for writing since an early age. He tends to write poetry and general fiction with an affinity for Horror and Sci-Fi. His second greatest fear is his lingering, perpetual existential crisis during which he contemplates the impermanence of reality. His greatest fear is spiders.

Amazon: www.amazon.com/author/joshuaslone
Twitter: @joshybo7
Facebook: www.facebook.com/joshuabslone

CPSIA information can be obtained at www.ICGtesting.com
Printed in the USA
LVOW11s0234150815

450250LV00005B/627/P